This Little Hippo
book belongs to

For Sophie Taylor.
D.B.

For V.
S.C.

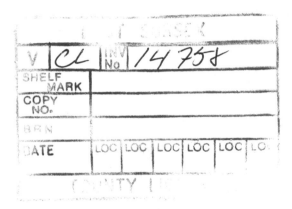

Scholastic Children's Books,
Commonwealth House, 1-19 New Oxford Street,
London WC1A 1NU, UK
a division of Scholastic Ltd

London • New York • Toronto • Sydney • Auckland
Mexico City • New Delhi • Hong Kong

First published by Little Hippo, an imprint of Scholastic Ltd, 2000

Text copyright © Denis Bond, 2000
Illustrations copyright © Steve Cox, 2000

ISBN 0 439 01458 1

Printed by Amadeus, Italy

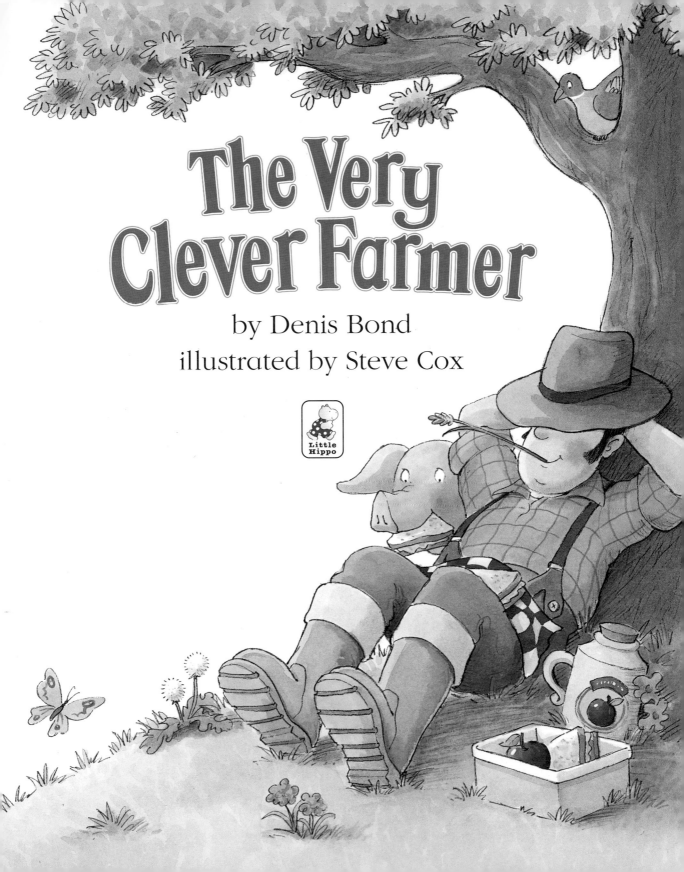

The Very Clever Farmer

by Denis Bond

illustrated by Steve Cox

Little Hippo

In a small, cosy farmhouse in the middle of the countryside, there lived a farmer.

The farmer had a wife and . . .

. . . one

two

three

four

. . . FIVE children.

He was a very clever farmer. He knew
everything about everything. Well, almost.

He could dance and he could sing. He was good at tennis . . . and even better at football. He was a great swimmer and a brilliant poet.

He could juggle and walk on stilts.

He knew how to mend a car and he thought that cooking spaghetti bolognese was easy-peasy.

In the evenings, he told stories to his five
children about scary monsters, nasty witches
and wondrous dragons. He was such
a good storyteller.

He was such a clever farmer.
He was good at everything
. . . well almost.

There was one thing
he couldn't do.

He couldn't count.

On the farm there were lots of sheep and as they leapt over the gate into their field, the farmer tried to count them.

"One . . . two . . . four . . . seven . . . eighteen . . . NINE!" he said.

"Dad," one of his little boys whispered, "we've got TWENTY-FOUR sheep."

"Oops!" grinned the farmer. "Silly me. Of course. Yes. Twenty-four sheep. I'll go and count the pigs," he said, quickly.

The farmer had lots of pigs. As they went into their pigsty in twos, he tried to count them.

"Two . . . four . . . seven . . . nine . . . three . . . THIRTEEN!" he said.

"Dad," one of his little girls whispered, "we've got TEN pigs."

"Oops!" smiled the farmer. "Silly me. Of course. Yes. Ten pigs," he said.

There were lots of chickens, pecking and scratching all over the farmyard. The clever farmer tried to count them.

"One . . . two . . . three . . . eight . . . five . . . nine . . . FOUR HUNDRED AND NINETY-TWO!" he said.

"Dad," one of his little boys whispered, "we've got TWENTY chickens."

"Oops!" giggled the farmer. "Silly me. Of course. Yes. Twenty chickens."

On his days off, the clever farmer painted
wonderful pictures. He mixed blue paint
with yellow paint to make green paint.
  He mixed red paint with blue paint to
make purple paint.
  He was a very clever farmer.

He knew that birds need wings to fly.
He knew that leaves grow on trees; that
cut grass always grows again; that pigs
eat anything, including your picnic; and
that no one will ever reach the end of the
rainbow, no matter how hard they try.

He was such a clever farmer.

One day the farmer took his family to the seaside. He bought an ice cream for each of his five children . . . and an ice lolly for his wife.

He counted out the money for the ice cream seller, "Five pence, two pence, fifty pence . . . TEN pence!"

The ice cream seller frowned and coughed politely.

"Dad," whispered the farmer's eldest daughter. "You haven't given him enough."

"Oops," said the farmer. "Silly me. Of course I haven't."

And he gave the ice cream seller some more money.

Two days later, it was the farmer's youngest son's birthday. The children left the farmyard and climbed on to the school bus. The farmer waved them goodbye. His wife went out shopping.

"Don't buy a birthday cake, dear," the farmer said. "I'll make one."

The farmer put a big mixing bowl on the table and began to make the cake. First he needed six large spoons of flour.

"One . . . two . . . seven . . . twenty-one . . . four . . . nine . . . eighteen . . . twelve . . . forty-two . . . SIX!" he said. "There! Six large spoons of flour. Easy!"

Next he needed three eggs.
"One . . . two . . . seventeen . . . five . . .
eight . . . twenty-six . . . nine . . . THREE!"
he said. "There! Three eggs. Easy!"

The farmer stirred the cake, put it into
a baking tin and popped it in the oven.
Then he went out to feed his animals.

But the cake had far too much flour in it . . . and it had far too many eggs in it. As it baked, it grew bigger and bigger and bigger, until suddenly, it burst through the oven door with a loud **BANG!**

Then it grew and grew and grew . . .

It filled the kitchen and spread into the lounge. It covered the sofa and the TV and the windows. Nothing was safe; not the cat nor the goldfish, nor the farmer's best wellies.

When the farmer's wife arrived home from the shops, she couldn't believe her eyes.

Cake was oozing from the windows, squidging through the chimney and squelching off the rooftop.

"Oops!" said the farmer, as he came in from the fields.

The farmer shovelled, and swept, and scrubbed and polished, while his wife rushed out to buy a birthday cake. And when the children arrived home from school, they had a lovely birthday party for their six-year old brother.

During the holidays, the farmer played hide-and-seek with his five children.

"You all run and hide." he said. "I'll count to ten . . . then I'll come and find you." And the clever farmer counted, "One . . . two . . . eighteen . . . fifty-four . . . seven . . . sixty-two . . ."

But by the time he'd reached ten, the children had given up waiting for him and gone off to watch television instead.

"Oops!" said the farmer.
"Never mind, Dad," said his middle daughter. "We'll play again tomorrow."

Six weeks later, the farmer made the worst mistake of all! On his way home from market, he decided to buy presents for his five children. And as he handed them out, he counted, "One . . . two . . . twenty-six . . . fifteen . . . oops!"

There was nothing for his youngest daughter. She burst into tears!

"Oh dear," said the farmer. "Everything seems to go wrong, just because I can't count." He felt very sad.

"You're never too old to learn, Dad," said his six-year old son.

"But how?" said the farmer. His smallest son giggled and whispered in his ear.

"RIGHT!" agreed the farmer.

The next morning, the farmer followed his one . . . two . . . three . . . four . . . five children on to the school bus.

"I'm going to school!" he said. "I'm going to learn to count."

Three weeks later, the clever farmer counted things all the way home from school. "Five trees, one postman, two cars, six bicycles, three cats . . ."

"Counting is easy!" he yelled at the top of his voice. "Ten flowers, two dogs, five children and . . . one wife!" he laughed.

Today the farmer is back on his farm, with his sheep and his pigs. He still dances and paints and walks on stilts. He still swims and plays football and makes spaghetti bolognese. And he still tells fantastic stories to his children.

But now, he can count as well. And that makes him a very happy, very clever farmer!